LEGITIMATE NEWS SOURCES

by A. W. Buckey

BrightPoint Press

San Diego, CA

BrightP◆int Press

© 2022 BrightPoint Press
an imprint of ReferencePoint Press, Inc.
Printed in the United States

For more information, contact:
BrightPoint Press
PO Box 27779
San Diego, CA 92198
www.BrightPointPress.com

LIBRARY OF CONGRESS CATALOGING-IN-PUBLICATION DATA

Names: Buckey, A. W., author.
Title: Legitimate news sources / A. W. Buckey.
Description: San Diego, CA : BrightPoint Press, an imprint of ReferencePoint Press, Inc.,
    [2022] | Series: Media literacy | Includes bibliographical references and index. | Audience:
    Grades 7-9
Identifiers: LCCN 2021011309 (print) | LCCN 2021011310 (eBook) | ISBN 9781678202026
    (hardcover) | ISBN 9781678202033 (eBook)
Subjects: LCSH: Media literacy--Juvenile literature. | Journalism--Objectivity--Juvenile
    literature.
Classification: LCC P96.M4 B83 2022 (print) | LCC P96.M4 (eBook) | DDC 302.23--dc23
LC record available at https://lccn.loc.gov/2021011309
LC eBook record available at https://lccn.loc.gov/2021011310

CONTENTS

AT A GLANCE

- Good news informs people about what's going on. It avoids presenting information in a biased way.

- All cultures use news. It helps people understand each other and the world. However, there's a long history of misleading news. Some news seeks to persuade, anger, or fool the audience.

- In the United States, TV and internet news are very popular. Many people get their news from social media too. But they should be careful about news coming from social media platforms. Some stories could come from illegitimate sources. They could have false information.

- Legitimate news sources have professional staff. They also have good reputations. These news sources have systems in place for making trustworthy stories.

- No news source is free of mistakes and bias. But legitimate news sources admit mistakes. They print corrections. They work hard to not write with bias.

- Illegitimate news sources print fake news. They write with bias. They also twist the facts. Illegitimate news sources may exist to make money. They may also be trying to promote an agenda.

- People can look out for the common signs of illegitimate news. Strange URLs, grammar mistakes, and emotional language are signs of illegitimate online news.

UNCOVERING GOOD SOURCES

S am flipped open his laptop. It was time for him to do a report for his environmental science class. Sam had picked a topic that hit close to home. Last month, the mayor announced that a paper company had decided to build a factory in town. She said the factory would create a lot of new jobs. However, an environmental

Using good sources in school reports is one step toward getting good grades.

group called Save Our Water immediately

started **protesting**. The group said the

paper factory would **pollute** the local river.

Sam needed to know if that was true.

Sam started with a simple Google search. He typed in the name of his town and the phrase "new paper factory." A few results came up. One was from the *Chicago Tribune*. Sam knew that was a big newspaper with a good reputation. But the article was too short to help much.

He started looking for articles about Save Our Water. He found a website with a weird URL. It ended with "co/inf" instead of "com." Sam frowned. He knew that an unusual URL could be a sign of a fake news site. In addition, an article on the site made some bold claims about Save Our Water.

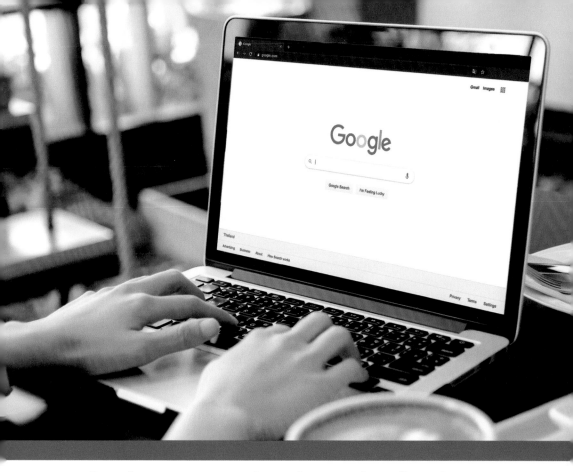

People can use search engines, such as Google, from computers or smart devices.

"Save Our Water is the secret enemy of the town," it said. Sam had his doubts about the source.

Finally, Sam discovered an article from his city's paper. The article quoted some locals who supported the new factory and some who were against it. And it revealed an interesting fact. A government report found that the same paper company had polluted a river in a different town. Sam started typing up what he learned. He felt like he was getting closer to the truth.

GOOD INFORMATION COMES FROM GOOD SOURCES

People may struggle to find reliable information, especially online. They use the news to feel connected to current events, form opinions, and make important decisions. But there is a lot of news, and

People get their news from online sources, newspapers, television, and other forms of media.

not all of it is trustworthy. Good news

sources have to tell the truth and represent

multiple perspectives. This can be a difficult

but important task. Finding reliable and fair

information starts with finding a legitimate

news source.

CHAPTER ONE

WHAT IS A LEGITIMATE NEWS SOURCE?

The news aims to report just the facts about situations. Sometimes journalists write stories about things that happened several years previously. And important or complex news stories can include historical details as context. But oftentimes, the goal

Journalists often report on topics that affect a lot of people.

of news is to tell people what's going on at the moment.

News sources are professional organizations that create and release news.

News comes in several formats. Print, or written, news is published in newspapers, in magazines, and on websites. Audio news comes in radio or podcast formats. Video news appears on TV stations or in online videos.

NON-NEWS IN NEWSPAPERS AND MAGAZINES

Not everything that appears in a news source is news. Newspapers and magazines usually make money by selling advertising space to companies. These advertisements are not news. In addition, newspapers often include opinion sections. They focus on people's arguments and opinions rather than reporting. Other common features that are not news include cartoons and puzzles.

All news has an audience. Not everyone is interested in the same topics or events. Different outlets provide news that varies based on the audience's language, location, identity, and interests. Some news audiences are very large. For example, the British Broadcasting Corporation (BBC) is a news organization in the United Kingdom. It reaches an international audience. The BBC provides news in more than forty languages to more than 250 million people. Other news sources are designed for specific groups. For example, many middle and high schools have their own newspapers.

MEDIA BIAS CHART

Left	Leans Left	Center	Leans Right	Right
BuzzFeed News	ABC News	BBC	The American Conservative	The American Spectator
CNN	The Atlantic	The Hill	The Dispatch	The Blaze
HuffPost	CBS News	Market Watch	Fox News (news pieces)	The Federalist
MSNBC	The Guardian	Newsweek	New York Post (news pieces)	Fox News (opinion pieces)
The New York Times (opinion pieces)	NBC News	Reuters	Washington Examiner	National Review
The New Yorker	The New York Times (news pieces)	USA Today	The Washington Times	New York Post (opinion pieces)
Slate	Time			
Vox	The Washington Post			

News organizations sometimes target certain audiences. For instance, some news sites cater to Democratic ideas. Others focus on Republican ones. Some news sources are more biased than others. Democratic views are called the "left," and Republican views are called the "right." The organization All Sides created a chart showing which way it thinks some news sources lean.

These sources publish news that's relevant to people at the school.

HOW IS NEWS CREATED?

The process of making news is called reporting. People who do this work are called reporters or journalists. Reporters try to answer six basic questions: Who? What? When? Where? Why? How? To get truthful answers to these questions, reporters go as close to the event as they can.

Imagine a large fire started at a town's busiest restaurant. A reporter covering the event couldn't rely on rumors to get the story. She would travel to the restaurant to get a closer look. If she arrived after

the fire was put out, she would interview

people who were there when it started.

She would ask the witnesses to tell her

when the fire began and how big it got.

BEAT REPORTING

Most large news sources report on several different topics at one time. Often, a reporter will specialize in one topic. This special focus is called a beat. Crime, local government, and sports are all examples of common news beats. Beat reporters get to know many sources within their special focus. For example, a basketball reporter can build relationships with teams and players. He can also be familiar with coaches, team owners, and fans. These relationships make stories easier to report.

The reporter would use these interviews in her story. She would quote the witnesses. In addition, the reporter would try to figure out why the fire started in the first place. She would learn how first responders dealt with the fire and the damage it caused. She might reach out to a fire safety expert for more information.

In this way, reporters rely on witnesses, quotes, firsthand knowledge, and experts to make news. Diana Moskovitz is a journalist. She writes about sports and crime. She explained that reporters must work hard to find good information. "Want to talk to

Journalists often record what witnesses or experts say. That way, they can listen to the recordings when putting stories together.

someone? Ask them for an interview. Want

that police report? Ask for a copy of it.

Want that video? Ask for a copy of that too,"

Moskovitz said.[1]

Most events never end up on the news. Reporters must consider which stories to publish. A story worth sharing is described as newsworthy. According to the news channel PBS, the elements of newsworthiness are timeliness, proximity, conflict and controversy, human interest, and relevance. So, a newsworthy story usually has happened recently. It typically occurs close to where the news audience lives. Issues that people argue about and reports of war and conflict are newsworthy. So are stories about interesting, unusual people, and stories that are useful to readers.

WHAT MAKES A NEWS SOURCE LEGITIMATE?

A legitimate news source is one that is fair and trustworthy. Legitimate news sources follow a reliable news-making process. They look for newsworthy stories and use careful reporting to answer the six questions. A legitimate news source does not make up information or spread rumors and gossip.

All news sources have to deal with the problem of bias. This is a tendency toward a certain point of view. Everyone has feelings,

People's biases about certain topics can sometimes trigger arguments.

thoughts, and judgments that affect the way they see the world. Some of these biases are easy to spot. For example, some people love baseball, and others find the sport boring. Other biases can be more difficult to identify. They come from the limits of each person's experience and perspective.

Imagine that a reporter from the United States is working on a story about a disagreement between the US and Bulgarian governments. The reporter may not have any prejudices against Bulgaria or its government. Even so, few Americans can speak or read Bulgarian. An American reporter will probably find it much easier to interview US government officials than Bulgarian ones. He will probably better understand the history and context behind the United States' side of the argument. These factors can lead to a kind of hidden bias. The reporter may focus more on the

Reporters often try to create well-rounded stories for their audiences, but sometimes their biases show.

parts of the story he understands or is

interested in. He may report biased news

without even realizing it.

AVOIDING BIAS

Legitimate news sources try to be as

objective as possible. Objective means

free of bias. News sources avoid obvious bias by leaving personal opinions out of news stories. Stories are usually reported in neutral language. That means reporters do not use certain words that might persuade people to think a certain way. For example, imagine that a reporter is quoting someone. A neutral word that could be used after the quote would be *said*. This term is less charged than words such as *ranted* or *whined*. Those two terms may show a reporter's bias toward the speaker.

In addition, reporters sometimes deliver the news in an unemotional tone to mask their own thoughts. Legitimate news sources also work to represent multiple viewpoints in a story. This helps keep the story objective.

PROPAGANDA AND NEWS

Propaganda strongly promotes certain viewpoints. It is sometimes used by governments and political parties. Propaganda can take many forms. It can be seen in movies, posters, books, and more. It is sometimes published as news. One clue that a story is propaganda instead of news is the type of language used. Propaganda tries to stir up emotions such as fear, pride, and hate. To avoid being tricked by propaganda, people can look out for simple language with lots of emotional words.

CHAPTER TWO

WHAT IS THE HISTORY OF JOURNALISM STANDARDS?

People value information about current events. News warns people of incoming dangers. It can help people make important decisions. News lets people know what's going on with others and the world. It's been around for thousands of

Newspapers have been around for centuries. Some people still rely on them today.

years. Mitchell Stephens is a historian. He said, "Humans have exchanged a similar mix of news . . . throughout history and across cultures."[2]

The first written news appeared in ancient Rome around 59 BCE. It also appeared in China around 618 CE. Both these large empires created newsletters. The letters had reports of powerful people's decisions and activities.

The first newspapers that were regularly printed appeared in central Europe in the early 1600s. The practice of making newspapers spread across Europe. In the mid-1800s, the electric telegraph was invented. It used electric wires to send messages across long distances. Telegraphs let reporters cover more news

Telegraph operators deciphered Morse code coming over telegraphs.

stories quickly and accurately. Reporters

could contact faraway witnesses in minutes

instead of days. The telegraph led to the

creation of wire service companies. Wire

services would collect news from around

the world. They would send it by telegraph to newspapers. Two of the first wire services were Reuters and the Associated Press. They are still active today.

YELLOW JOURNALISM AND JOURNALISM STANDARDS

In the late 1800s, a battle started in the US newspaper business. Two wealthy men, William Randolph Hearst and Joseph Pulitzer, both owned New York City newspapers. They competed fiercely for the biggest audience. Their newspapers looked for stories that would shock and surprise people. Many stories had exciting and

The printing press allowed people to make a large number of papers at affordable prices.

exaggerated details. Some were completely

made up. This type of reporting became

known as yellow journalism.

The two newspapers even published

fake stories that preyed on people's

Newsboys would sell newspapers on the streets.

biases. For instance, both men saw that

anti-Spanish stories sold well with readers.

In 1898, a US ship exploded in Cuba.

Hearst and Pulitzer suggested Spanish

forces destroyed it. In reality, the explosion

was probably an accident. Rumor says Hearst once told an illustrator, "You furnish the pictures, I'll furnish the war."[3] In other words, Hearst thought a few illustrations showing what happened in Cuba would help sell his biased, dishonest news to readers. The US government eventually went to war with Spain.

The yellow journalism trend helped increase the US news audience. But readers began trusting the news less and less. Journalists wanted to change the business. Starting around 1900, journalists started making their own ethical codes and standards. Experts created the first journalism guides and classes. The journalism profession improved its reputation for honesty and careful work.

PUBLIC RELATIONS AND PRESS RELEASES

In the early 1900s, a journalist named Ivy Lee changed jobs. He realized many businesses feared the news media. When companies made mistakes, they would try to stop reporters from finding out.

Lee decided to use a different approach. When businesses had problems or accidents, Lee wrote his own report of what happened. Then he gave this report

People hired to make press releases are paid to portray information about a subject in a certain light.

to journalists to print in newspapers. In this

way, Lee created the press release. These

releases aim to give companies more

control over their news coverage.

Today, companies, governments, universities, and famous people commonly use press releases. Releases include quotes that journalists can use in their reporting. For example, Netflix is a popular video-streaming company. It operates in more than 190 countries. Netflix publishes press releases about its business and creative decisions. In January 2021, Netflix put out a press release celebrating the success of a newly released TV show on its service. Netflix vice president of original series Jinny Howe wrote it. Hundreds of news sources quoted or rephrased Howe's

Press releases can be published both online and in print.

words in their own reports. Press releases,

like news, should be factual. But they are

made to promote a biased perspective.

RADIO, TV, AND INTERNET NEWS

Radio broadcasting was invented in the

1920s. It allowed for the first audio news

programs. In the 1930s, the lead-up to World War II (1939–1945) got many more Americans interested in international news. People liked hearing live reports instead of waiting for the paper. As a result, radio news jumped in popularity.

Television became widespread after World War II. At first, there were just a few popular TV stations. All of them had regular news broadcasts. By the 1960s, TV news became more popular. That's because reporters could cover events as they happened. And millions of people watched news anchors each night. Anchors became public figures. People had a lot of faith in them. For example, Walter Cronkite was a news anchor. In the 1960s and 1970s, some people called him "the most trusted man in America."[4]

THE FREEDOM OF INFORMATION ACT

The Freedom of Information Act (FOIA) is a US law. It was created in 1967. It allows US citizens to look at documents from government agencies. For example, a journalist writing a story on public schools can ask the Department of Education for some of its records. Asking for this information is called making a FOIA request. Usually, the US government is required to fulfill FOIA requests. But there are exceptions. Sensitive information, like national security records, is sometimes kept private.

In the 1990s, print news sources started publishing some stories online. The internet became more popular. Many people switched from newspapers to online news. There is a huge amount of information on

DEFAMATION, SLANDER, AND LIBEL

Defamation is a legal term for a damaging, false statement. *Slander* is a spoken defamatory statement. *Libel* is written defamation. People or companies that believe they have been defamed can go to court. News organizations must be careful. They want to avoid defamation in reporting. They typically use the word *alleged* when talking about crimes and people who've been arrested. This is partly because suspects could sue for defamation if found not guilty.

the internet. This makes news easier to get than ever before. The Pew Research Center did a survey in 2020. It found that more than 80 percent of Americans either frequently or sometimes got news from a smart device or computer. About half watched TV news often. Social media services such as Twitter, Facebook, and Instagram let users share and promote news. Many people get news on social media. But not everyone trusts these sources. The Pew Research Center found that more than half of social media users thought the news on social media was not accurate.

CHAPTER THREE

WHAT KINDS OF NEWS SOURCES ARE AVAILABLE TODAY?

News organizations that are **reputable** have a history

of providing accurate news. News

organizations of any size can have good,

reliable news. But it's easiest to check

the reputations of older and larger news

Many people watch nightly news programs to get accurate information.

sources. Large newspapers, wire services,

and major TV news programs have large

audiences. If they have untruthful news,

people will notice. This is especially true

when it comes to major news stories.

For instance, imagine that a large volcano suddenly erupts in the United States. The next day, a major newspaper reports on the event. The paper's story gets some basic facts wrong, like where the eruption happened. Many readers spot the newspaper's mistake. In the future, they'll be less likely to trust the paper. To avoid factual mistakes, large news outlets spend money on editing, fact-checking, and research.

Each news source has a different audience. Therefore, news sources often reflect the biases of their readers, listeners, and viewers. This does not mean the

People rely on reporters to give them updates on breaking news stories.

news is false. But it may be slanted in its

presentation. People can try searching

online for a news source's name and

the word *bias*. The results should give

some clues about the source's audience

and reputation.

Large news sources have more

resources and accountability. But smaller

news sources are sometimes more likely to report reliably. For example, industry publications have in-depth news related to their fields. A newsletter for veterinarians could publish a very detailed story on medication for horses. A larger news source would not publish the same story. Not enough people in their audience would have the knowledge and interest needed to read it. In the same way, a local news outlet can report on stories that a large one might overlook or misunderstand. A school newspaper, for example, has a very limited audience. But the student

Students work together to create school newspapers.

reporters understand the school. They also understand their peers in a way that outside reporters don't. This insider knowledge can give legitimacy to stories.

NO NEWS SOURCE IS TOTALLY ACCURATE

No news source will always get it right. Mistakes, biases, and dishonesty can happen at any point in the process. Sometimes legitimate news sources are fooled by witnesses and experts. For example, a professor named Joseph Boskin once made up a story about how April Fools' Day was created. He told a reporter a long, fake story. It was about an ancient jester. The journalist believed Boskin. He printed the story for his wire service. Several other newspapers followed with the same

Journalists should think carefully about whether people they interview are reliable sources of information.

story. It was weeks before Boskin finally told

the truth. His prank was pretty harmless.

But it demonstrated the fact that journalists

cannot rely on one person's word. Raul

Ramirez is a news director. He said, "Until

we figure a way to look into people's hearts, journalists would be ill advised to believe absolutely what any source says at all times."[5]

Dishonest journalists can also mislead people. For example, Brian Williams was

CONFLICT OF INTEREST

In news, a conflict of interest happens when a reporter's outside life clashes with her ability to write fairly. A reporter should be honest about any conflicting interest. Otherwise, her story could be biased. For example, a crime journalist should not report on a relative's trial. A conflict of interest can also occur at the business level. For instance, Jeff Bezos is the founder of Amazon. He also owns the *Washington Post*. Reporters for the *Washington Post* must think carefully about how they report on Amazon.

an anchor for NBC Nightly News. In 2015, he was called out for lying. Years before, Williams said he was in a helicopter that was forced to land after being shot at in Iraq. But he was actually in a different helicopter. Williams's lie showed he was an unreliable witness to a news event. Williams was suspended from his job for six months.

Reliable news sources may rush to publish stories. This can lead to sloppy journalism. For instance, the *New York Times* has a good reputation. It's seen as one of the top newspapers in the United States. However, in 2004 the

New York Times apologized to its readers. The editors admitted that the paper made many errors in its coverage of the US decision to invade Iraq in 2003. People were not careful about checking the information they printed on the topic. The *New York Times* reported claims about weapons of mass destruction in Iraq. These turned out to be false. As the newspaper explained, "editors at several levels who should have been challenging reporters and pressing for more skepticism were perhaps too intent on rushing scoops into the paper."[6]

Some journalists enter war zones to report what's going on there.

All news sources are imperfect. But when a legitimate news source makes a mistake, it responds responsibly. For example, news outlets issue corrections when they get story details wrong.

ILLEGITIMATE NEWS SOURCES AND WHY THEY EXIST

A news source that often has false content or is openly biased is illegitimate. There are many motivations for posting fake stories.

NEWS SOURCES AND CONSPIRACY THEORIES

Some people believe in conspiracy theories. They think hidden groups are secretly behind world events. News sources sometimes report on conspiracy theories. This happens if the theories start having real-world effects. For instance, believers of the theories may start acting on those beliefs. But legitimate news does not promote conspiracies. Legitimate news sources only make claims they can support with evidence. They must not hint at secret plans without proof.

One is money. As yellow journalism proved, untrustworthy news can be exciting to read. People are often willing to pay for surprising and entertaining news. Yellow journalism continues today. It can be found in printed sources. It's also on websites with shocking headlines and pictures.

Illegitimate news sources may also have biased **agendas**. For example, many illegitimate news sources try to promote political goals. Spreading false information may influence people's voting decisions. In 2016, Donald Trump and Hillary Clinton were running for president. False stories about them appeared on Facebook. Tens of millions of people shared these stories. Some of the fake news authors were people looking to make money. Others wanted to influence people's votes. Fake news can also stir existing political tensions.

WHY IS WIKIPEDIA NOT A LEGITIMATE NEWS SOURCE?

Wikipedia is a huge information resource. The information found there is often accurate and well sourced. Even so, Wikipedia is not a legitimate news source. That's because Wikipedia and sites like it are not news sources at all. Reporters create news by interviewing sources.

They do original research. The news they

create is a primary source. Wikipedia is a

secondary source. It gets information from

primary sources, such as news articles.

Secondary sources can be useful. But they

are not substitutes for news.

SNOPES

Snopes.com is a website. It fact-checks stories on the internet. These stories can be from legitimate news sources. Or they can come from personal websites, email chains, or fake news sites. David Mikkelson started Snopes in the 1990s. Today, the site has multiple editors. Snopes is not a news source, but it uses a research process similar to reporting.

CHAPTER FOUR

HOW CAN I FIND TRUSTWORTHY NEWS SOURCES?

Media literacy is the ability to understand and interpret different types of media. These can include newspapers and TV broadcasts. Strong media literacy skills make it easier to find and use legitimate news sources. These skills develop through practice. Checking

People should think critically about their news sources.

the news every day is a good start. It's

a way for people to get a feel for good

news stories. People can develop a strong

knowledge of current events. That way, it's

easier to tell truth from lies in the news.

People can try picking a few large news sources to check regularly. They can see how different outlets cover the same story. This can help train people to find biases. They may also notice differences in perspective. It can also help to follow a favorite interest, such as video games, in the news. It's easier to spot mistakes when the news subject is something familiar.

RESEARCH ON THE INTERNET

News research tends to start on the internet. There's a lot of legitimate news online. But there's illegitimate news too. Internet search engines aren't perfect.

Each search engine has a slightly different system for ordering its results. It's not a search engine's job to make sure a news source is legitimate.

However, it's often better to find online news using a search engine than social

---

SPONSORED CONTENT

Sponsored content is a type of advertising. It typically appears on websites. This includes online news sources. Sponsored content imitates the format of the regular content on the website. For example, the website BuzzFeed publishes news. But it also has opinion pieces, gossip, quizzes, and other articles. Sponsored content on BuzzFeed is paid for by a company. However, it's designed to look like other BuzzFeed articles. Sponsored content is not objective, and it is not news.

media. Social media platforms make money by getting as much attention from users as possible. This leads to a bias toward attention-grabbing stories. Social media wants to engage a lot of people. Modern-day yellow journalism spreads on social media quickly. That's because the stories are dramatic. They catch people's attention. Then people share those stories. This spreads fake news.

It's important that people do some research on a news source before trusting its information. To do this, they can go to the "About" page of a news website.

Social Media

People can get their news from a lot of different social media services. But not all of this news is legitimate.

This page gives information about who runs the site. If a website doesn't have an "About" section, it's a red flag. The site may not be legitimate.

Sometimes it's not clear whether a news source is publishing legitimate stories. People can look for stories on subjects they know a lot about. For example, a reader who knows a lot about the stock market can check out stories about that. Are the facts right? Does the source seem biased?

In addition, people should be cautious when they see websites with strange URLs. Illegitimate news websites often use URLs similar to those of existing news sites. But they change a few letters. Other clues include spelling and grammar mistakes in stories. The formatting in stories might seem strange too. Professional news

sources try to avoid language mistakes

and poor designs. And when in doubt,

Common Sense Media says, "Check your

emotions. . . . If the news you're reading

DEEPFAKES

A deepfake is a photo or video that has been changed. Deepfakes use complex computer technology. They replace human faces on existing images. Deepfake technology raises two major news concerns. First, audiences can be tricked into thinking a fake photo or video is real. The second danger is that people might believe real videos are in fact deepfakes. People are researching ways to detect deepfakes accurately. In early 2020, Facebook banned misleading deepfake videos.

makes you really angry or super smug, it could be a sign that you're being played."[7]

FOLLOWING THE TRAIL OF NEWS

To find legitimate news, people should develop certain **habits**. They can look carefully at a story to see if a reporter interviewed witnesses. They can see if the story has expert quotes or if the story is showing different viewpoints. People can check whether information and quotes come from press releases, original reporting, or both. One well-researched news story can lead the way to others. For example, many reporters write multiple stories on the same topic. If people find a good news story on one topic, they can check out the author. They may want to read more articles written by this person.

REPORTING ON SCIENCE TOPICS

News sources may misrepresent scientific research. They may stretch the truth to make it seem exciting or relevant. James Heathers is a scientist. He kept track of scientific studies on mice. Many news sources reported on these studies. Heathers found many examples where the news sources exaggerated the scientific findings. In many cases, headlines made it seem like the studies were about humans. People should be careful of news headlines that make broad scientific claims. They should also check to make sure experts are quoted.

People can also try looking up the individuals quoted in the story. Are they experts on the topic or event? If so, they may be quoted in other news sources too. For example, in 2020 the disease COVID-19 started spreading around the globe. It caused a worldwide **pandemic**. During this time, a small group of medical experts spoke to multiple news outlets. Experts want to give good information. They prefer to speak to legitimate news sources. A news source that quotes real experts is more likely to be legitimate.

Experts told people to wear face masks in public during the pandemic. This helped slow the spread of COVID-19.

It can be useful to look at several news sources when researching a topic. For instance, imagine that someone is trying to get news on a recent Supreme Court case. Most large US news sources would probably cover the story. The Supreme Court also has its own press releases. News sources made for lawyers give more detailed news on legal matters. And local news sources might give a totally different perspective. Looking at all these news sources could give a reader a well-rounded view of the topic.

THE POWER OF SHARING NEWS

There are many ways for people to identify which news sources are legitimate. People can also figure out which stories have biases. They can identify which news is fake. This can prevent them from believing

By looking critically at news sources, people can stop themselves from sharing false content.

lies. People who understand the news can play powerful roles. They can share good news stories with others. They can also educate people on media literacy skills. These skills can help everyone find legitimate news sources.

GLOSSARY

agendas

motivations or intentions of a certain person or group

habits

practices or tendencies people develop that are hard to break

pandemic

an outbreak of a disease that spreads across the globe

pollute

to make something unclean

propaganda

information that is created and spread to influence an audience to think a certain way

protesting

expressing disapproval, sometimes through a public demonstration

reputable

having a good standing and trusted by many people

SOURCE NOTES

CHAPTER ONE: WHAT IS A LEGITIMATE NEWS SOURCE?

1. Diana Moskovitz, "14 Things I Wish I Knew Before I Became an Investigative Reporter," *Cosmopolitan*, February 23, 2016. www.cosmopolitan.com.

CHAPTER TWO: WHAT IS THE HISTORY OF JOURNALISM STANDARDS?

2. Quoted in Bill Kovach and Tom Rosenstiel, *The Elements of Journalism: What Newspeople Should Know and the Public Should Expect*. New York: Three Rivers Press, 2012, p. 2.

3. Quoted in "Yellow Journalism: William Randolph Hearst," *PBS*, n.d. www.pbs.org.

4. Quoted in "Walter Cronkite Biography," *PBS*, July 26, 2006. www.pbs.org.

CHAPTER THREE: WHAT KINDS OF NEWS SOURCES ARE AVAILABLE TODAY?

5. Quoted in Jeffery A. Dvorkin, "'Hello, Mom? What Makes a Source Reliable?'" *NPR*, November 15, 2005. www.npr.org.

6. Quoted in "From the Editors: *The Times* and Iraq," *New York Times*, May 26, 2004. www.nytimes.com.

CHAPTER FOUR: HOW CAN I FIND TRUSTWORTHY NEWS SOURCES?

7. Quoted in "How to Spot Fake News," *Common Sense Media*, March 5, 2021. www.commonsensemedia.org.

FOR FURTHER RESEARCH

BOOKS

Diane Dakers, *Information Literacy and Fake News*. New York: Crabtree
　　Publishing, 2018.

Tammy Gagne, *Identifying Media Bias*. San Diego, CA: BrightPoint
　　Press, 2022.

Duchess Harris, *The Fake News Phenomenon*. Minneapolis, MN: Abdo
　　Publishing, 2018.

INTERNET SOURCES

"Media," *Britannica Kids*, n.d. https://kids.britannica.com.

Kaiser Moffat, "The Importance of Media Literacy," *Young Leaders of the
　　Americas Initiative*, n.d. https://ylai.state.gov.

"Why Today's Students Need Media Literacy More Than Ever," *Fresno
　　Pacific University*, December 17, 2018. https://ce.fresno.edu.

WEBSITES

All Sides
www.allsides.com

All Sides looks at stories published by different news sources. It analyzes the stories and gives opinions on how balanced they are.

News Literacy Project: News Literacy Tips & Tools
https://newslit.org/tips-tools

News Literacy Tips & Tools provides quizzes and articles for people who want to develop their media literacy skills.

Web Evaluation & News Sources: Reputable News
https://libguides.ucmerced.edu/news/reputable

The University of California Merced gives information on how to find legitimate news sources and how to fact-check content. It provides examples of sponsored content to look out for.

INDEX

IMAGE CREDITS

ABOUT THE AUTHOR

A. W. Buckey is a writer and pet sitter living in Brooklyn, New York.